The Hit and Run GANG

YOU'RE OUT!

STEVEN KROLL grew up in New York City, where he was a pretty good first baseman and #3 hitter on baseball teams in Riverside Park. He graduated from Harvard University, spent almost seven years as an editor in book publishing, and then became a full-time writer. He is the author of more than fifty books for young people. He lives in New York City and roots for the Mets.

The Hit and Run GANG 6

YOU'RE OUT!

STEVEN KROLL

Illustrated by Meredith Johnson

AN AVON CAMELOT BOOK

THE HIT AND RUN GANG #6: YOU'RE OUT! is an original publication of Avon Books. This work has never before appeared in book form.

AVON BOOKS
A division of
The Hearst Corporation
1350 Avenue of the Americas
New York, New York 10019

First Avon Camelot Printing: March 1994

For Patti Hassett

Contents

1. A Gloomy Day

It was a damp, cold, misty afternoon, but it wasn't quite bad enough for Ron Channing, head coach and manager of the Raymondtown Rockets, to call off practice.

So the team was all there, going through the motions at the ballfield down behind the IGA. They'd warmed up and gone through sliding and baserunning drills. With coaches Carr and Lopez looking on, they'd divided into groups of four and played outfielder, relay man, hitter, and catcher. Then they'd rotated those positions to give everyone a chance to play everywhere.

Now the starters were in their positions in the field. Coach Channing was at the plate, fungoing the ball and barking instructions about what to do. No one looked any happier than before, but ahead of each batted ball, the players bent their knees, got up on the balls of their feet, kept their gloves in front of them. There was a home game tomorrow with the Panthers, and they wanted to be sharp.

Out in center field, Michael Wong was doing his best to stay involved. He'd made a good catch on a fly ball over his head, sighting it well and pulling it in before it reached the fence. He'd backed up Pete Wyshansky on a fly to right. But the truth was, Michael wasn't feeling very well. He had a cold, which he'd told no one about, and the lousy weather had made it worse. Standing in position, in the middle of the outfield he loved so much, Michael wiped the mist off his face with his sleeve and hoped he didn't have a temperature. If he did, his mother would never let him play tomorrow.

"Runner on first, nobody out, get two, Phil," Coach Channing shouted.

He cracked a ground ball to Phil Hubbard at third base. Phil got down, got under it, looked the ball all the way into his glove, turned, and fired to Vicky Lopez at second. Vicky reached the bag at the same time as the ball, pivoted, and pegged a strike to Andy McClellan, who was

2

playing first because Justin Carr was on the mound.

"Good going, all three of you!" the coach yelled. "Now—one on, one out!"

A high fly ball to Jenny Carr, Justin's twin, in left. Jenny went back, back, got under it, and made the catch over her throwing shoulder. Then she strode forward and fired the ball to Vicky to hold the runner.

Michael was backing up the play. He returned to center field as Coach Channing shouted, "Well done, Jenny! Now, Michael, runner on first, two out."

A hard grounder came scorching up the middle. Michael charged it, the way he always did. He was proud of his speed, proud it could help him make hard plays look easy, but he ran sluggishly now, his nose stuffed up and his head full of cotton.

He got the ball in front of him, but he was running on his heels, not on the balls of his feet. He didn't get down far enough, didn't look the ball into his glove. It went through his legs.

Michael couldn't believe what he'd done. He

turned, picked up the ball, and hurled it to third, where it was supposed to keep the runner from advancing that far.

But the ball never reached Phil Hubbard at the bag. Michael forgot to plant his throwing-side foot and point his shoulder toward the target. The ball landed in the visitors' dugout.

Coach Channing said nothing. He walked over, retrieved the ball, and checked his watch. "We're a little short on time. Better get in some hitting."

Everyone stayed in position. One of the subs filled in for the player who was batting, and Andy and Justin shared the pitching. The order was the usual batting order, with the subs taking their licks at the end.

That meant Michael would be coming up eighth. He was hardly a big hitter, but he was proud of his good short stroke and his consistency. As Luke Emory, the Rockets' spark-plug catcher, led off, Michael hoped he would get a chance to make enough good plays to make everyone forget his errors and watch him hit.

On the very first pitch, Luke smacked a line drive to center. Michael caught it at the letters and pegged the ball to Justin. There. A good start. Keep them coming!

But they didn't keep coming. Luke hit a couple of flies to left and a grounder to Brian Krause at short. Phil didn't get a ball out of the infield. Andy's best shot was a line drive right at Vicky, and the rest of the crew seemed determined to go on missing, popping up, or grounding out. Justin powered one over Pete's head in right, but by the time Michael came in to hit, he hadn't had any more chances to show what he could do.

He found his bat and took a few practice swings. He knocked some dirt out of his sneakers with the head of the bat and stepped into the box. He anchored his rear foot, took a deep breath, got his arms back, and crouched.

His small size and his crouch narrowed his strike zone. He was as ready and determined as he'd ever be.

Justin wound and fired a fastball down and in. Michael swung early, missed, and went all the way around. The next pitch was a change-up, and Michael missed that, too.

"You're out in front," Coach Lopez warned. "Keep your eye on the ball."

"Come on, Michael," Luke said from behind him. "Just meet it, man. No need for over-hitting."

Michael blew his nose and settled in again. He adjusted his helmet, banged the bat on the plate, concentrated. He fouled off an across-the-seams fastball that tailed away over the plate, muscled a ground ball out to the mound, poked a base hit through the middle, and bunted foul twice toward first.

"You need to square around more quickly on the bunt," Coach Lopez said, "and bring those hands up farther on the bat."

Michael tried it. His last bunt was just fair along the third base line.

At least he got a piece of it going up the middle, at least that last bunt stayed fair, he thought, as he trudged back to center field.

2. Who's Cheering?

No one else did much better, but Michael couldn't help noticing when Adam Spinelli, always the best of the subs, belted two long balls off the fence in left.

Finally, practice was over. Coach Channing shook his head. "I know the weather is terrible, but I hope you've saved it all for tomorrow. We'll need some spark. Please get here early."

Everyone headed for the dugout. Michael got his gear together, then sat on the end of the bench for a moment before starting home. He couldn't have been more surprised when Coach Channing sat beside him.

"Can we talk a minute, Michael?"

"Sure, Coach."

The coach took off his cap and smoothed his dark hair. Then he put the cap back on again.

"You've done a fine job for us in center field,

and you've certainly hit more than adequately. But Adam Spinelli has been playing such excellent ball these past couple of weeks, I have to give him a chance. He'll start in center tomorrow and for the foreseeable future. Of course I'm sorry. We'll go game by game. I hope you understand."

Michael tried to remember when Adam had played so well. There was that game when he subbed for Brian at short and drove in a run, but that was the same game Michael hit his first double of the season. There were those two big hits today. . . .

"I'll be a substitute," Michael said, not knowing whether he was stating a fact or asking a question.

Coach Channing knit his brow. "Yes, that's right, but we'll get you as much playing time as we can."

Michael knew that didn't mean a lot. He looked straight ahead as the coach put his arm around him.

"I know you, Michael. You'll come out of this a better ballplayer. Wait and see."

Michael watched Coach Channing's retreating back. He was still sitting on the bench when Jenny, his best friend on the team, came over.

"What's the matter? You look like the world just fell in on you."

Michael was too ashamed to say it had. He had been a member of the starting team, and now he was not. His family would be upset. They would feel they had all been embarrassed. He almost wished he'd told the coach about his cold and how that and the weather had affected his playing, but that would have been making excuses.

Jenny sat down. "What's going on, Michael?"

Michael looked at her. He had to say something. He explained.

Jenny's jaw dropped. "I don't believe it. You're so much better than Adam Spinelli. Better hands, better glove, steadier bat. Sure, you made those errors today, but everyone was lousy today. The whole practice was awful."

"Two errors," Michael reminded her, "and a terrible piece of hitting." He sniffed. "And Adam got those two big hits."

Jenny scoffed at the comparison. "Remember when I made those *two* terrible errors in that game against the Tornadoes? Then I killed the rally that could have won it for us. Coach didn't take me off the starting team. All he did was encourage me. And you've been such a great team player. You've never even objected when you haven't started in the past."

A cheer went up outside the dugout. It was obviously followed by some high-fives.

"Coach Channing must have told Adam," Michael said.

Jenny looked closer. "Yeah, it's Luke, Phil, Brian, and Adam."

She poked Michael in the ribs. "Come on, Michael, you'll get your job back. I believe in you."

They walked off together. Coach Carr would drive Jenny and Justin home. Michael was going to walk.

As the Carr station wagon bounced out of the parking lot, Michael waved. He watched until the taillights disappeared into Market Street.

Then he started for home. It was true that

when Josh Rubin pitched, Andy frequently started in center field. Once or twice, Adam had subbed or even started for Michael. He'd never minded; he always thought first of the team and supporting the coach. But this was different. This was a real demotion.

Of course there was that horrendous error he'd made in the game against the Hurricanes a short while back, when Andy blew up afterwards and ran away from the team. On a pop-up behind second base, he ran right into Vicky Lopez backing up. She missed the ball, and the Hurricanes went on to a big inning. Coach Channing must have made up his mind then.

As Michael climbed the hill to his house, the sky was growing dark. It was useless to go on thinking about the team. His baseball career was ruined.

3. Room

Michael opened the door. No one. He walked into the kitchen and found his mother, his younger sister, Natalie, and his younger brother, David.

"Michael," his mother said, "we're glad you're home."

Michael smiled weakly.

"What's the matter? Are you sick?"

"It's just a cold. Practice made it worse."

"You shouldn't have been practicing with a cold. Straight to the shower and into bed. Then you'll have some ginseng root tea."

Michael went. The steam and the warmth of the water in the shower opened up his nose and throat. By the time he climbed into bed, he was actually feeling better.

His mother arrived with the tea. "If you

aren't well tomorrow, you'll have to stay home from the game.''

Michael leaned back against the pillows. ''It doesn't matter. I'm not starting anymore.''

''Oh?''

Michael described what had happened at practice and with Coach Channing. He kept his chin from trembling and knew he wouldn't cry.

Afterwards, his mother said, ''I see. I'm sorry.'' She hugged him. ''But first we must make you well.''

Michael drank his tea. His mother left the room, and he dozed. When he woke, she was there again, bringing his dinner on a tray.

He thanked her and sampled the bowl of rice with steamed fish and vegetables, but he wasn't very hungry. He turned out the light and let himself doze again as the dark surrounded him.

A while later, there was a knock on the door.

Michael sat up and turned on the light. ''Who is it?''

''Your father.''

''Please come in.''

The door opened. His father slipped into the

desk chair across the room. Gentle and serious, he was an architect in town.

There was a brief silence. Then he asked how Michael was feeling.

"Better, thanks," Michael said.

"What is this your mother tells me about the starting team?"

Michael's heart sank. In a low voice, he explained.

"I'm sorry," he said at the end. "I am the eldest son. I've disappointed the family."

His father said nothing. He seemed to disappear into the shadows across the room. Then he asked, "Did this happen because you're Chinese?"

The question was so far from Michael's mind, he was shocked. He thought about Coach Channing and the other members of the Rockets. "No," he said.

"I'm glad," said his father. "In that case, you must work twice as hard. Perhaps, once you have done that, you'll get back onto the starting team."

The words echoed what Jenny had said in the

dugout. Oddly, Michael realized, he'd been so upset by his fate, he hadn't even thought about trying to change it. Of course he would work harder. Of course he would get his job back. If only his father were more interested in baseball.

"Yes, Father," he said, and slid beneath the covers.

The door clicked shut. Michael dozed again. An hour or so later, there was another knock.

"Telephone, Michael," his mother said.

He pulled on his bathrobe and slippers and hurried to the phone in the kitchen. It had to be Jenny. Who else could it be?

"Hello?"

"Michael, it's Luke."

"Oh, hi."

"Listen, I hope I'm not calling at a bad time, but I wanted to apologize for what happened after practice this afternoon."

"Oh, that's okay."

"No, really, I mean it. That cheer and everything, I know it must have hurt you. I know it would have hurt me. We were just so pleased Adam would be starting, we got carried away.

I didn't want you to think it had anything to do with you.''

"I understand.''

"Great! So we'll see you at the game tomorrow?''

"Of course.''

When they had said their good-byes, Michael wandered back to his room. His confident "of course'' depended on what his mother said about his cold in the morning, but he had to be pleased that Luke had bothered to call.

There was a saying in Michael's family that only the nail that stood out got whacked. That was good advice, Michael thought. He wouldn't make a fuss, he would work very hard and start again in center field.

"I'm coming back,'' he said to his room.

4. Game Time

Michael fell into a deep sleep, a sleep he badly needed. He slept so well, his mother didn't wake him until after ten the next morning.

He sat up and stretched. His nose was no longer stuffed, his head had cleared. He felt like himself again and ready to greet the day.

"You seem better," his mother said.

"I *am* better!" Michael replied.

"We'll take your temperature first."

It was normal.

"Good," said Michael's mother. "You may play in the game this afternoon."

"Hooray!" said Michael.

Brushing his teeth in the bathroom, he remembered that he wouldn't be starting. Imagining this and the way things had changed made him dizzy. Perhaps he wouldn't get to play at all today. He could spend the whole game as a benchwarmer.

By the time he reached the kitchen, the morning was almost over. He had some juice and tea and a bun, and what seemed like moments later, it was time for lunch.

Afterwards, his father said, "I'm coming this afternoon."

Michael frowned without meaning to. "Even though I won't be starting?"

"Yes."

What a surprise. His father almost never came to games.

"I'm glad you're coming," Michael said. Then he ran back to his room and changed into his uniform.

The crisp white pants. The dark red shirt with the proud number 17 on the front. When he was dressed, he struck a pose in front of the mirror, something he would never do except in private. He had to admit it. He looked good.

The day was bright and clear, a perfect day for baseball. Down at the ballfield, Jenny hurried over.

"Are you okay?"

Michael shrugged. "My cold's gone. Luke called last night."

"No kidding. What did he say?"

Michael told her, and Jenny smiled. "That Luke. He's got more team spirit than anyone."

Coach Channing announced warm-ups. Michael threw himself into the stretches and wind sprints with new vigor. Then he attacked fielding and batting practice the same way.

If he was going to fight to get his job back, these were the places to start. Besides, it was Saturday. The stands were full of people eager for the game to begin. How could anyone not be enthusiastic?

With the Panthers taking practice, Coach Channing posted the lineup. Michael held back, waiting until the others had gone before he looked himself. For a moment he had a vain hope, but no, there it was, just as he'd been told: Batting eighth, Adam Spinelli, CF.

So the game began without him.

The Panthers were from the other side of

town. They were tough, and they swaggered. They wore black uniform shirts and black caps with a white Panther on the front. They also started out hot and heavy.

With his big, slow delivery, Justin pitched carefully, the way he always did, but he seemed a bit erratic coming in. Max Hobart, the Panthers' gruff shortstop lead-off man, leaned out over the plate and worked the count to 3 and 2. Then he got his pitch, a fastball down and away, and lashed a double over Vicky's head to center field.

Sitting on the bench, trying not to look like just another substitute, Michael wondered if Adam would misplay the ball. He didn't. He caught it cleanly on the big hop and fired it to third to hold the runner.

But second baseman Freddie Berman, a mean little contact hitter, was coming up. With the count 1 and 1, Hobart stole third on Justin's slow move to the plate. Then Berman belted a fastball to right and caught Pete playing shallow. The ball went over his head for an error and rolled to the fence.

Hobart came in to score. Before Pete could recover and heave the ball to Andy playing first, Berman was on third.

Usually unflappable, Justin squeezed the ball into his glove, toed the mound, fixed his cap.

"Come on, Justin, you can do it!" Michael yelled.

"Yeah, do it, yeah, do it," echoed back from the infield.

Already the crowd was quiet. Justin checked the runner, then wound and fired a fastball past burly Chuck Reese, the Panther first baseman.

"Strike 1!" the umpire yelled.

The crowd cheered. As if in response, Justin hurled another strike and coaxed a little nubbler out to the mound. He held the runner at third, then fired to Andy at first for the out.

But the Panthers weren't done. Their cleanup hitter, skinny Ben Lord, worked the count to 2 and 2.

"Stay in there!" someone yelled from the Panther bench, and Lord did exactly that. He turned on the next pitch and blasted a single to deep left, scoring Berman standing up despite

Jenny's perfect throw to Brian, the cut-off man, at short. The Panthers led 2–0 with only one out and the pitcher coming up.

The pitcher was a girl. Her name was Angela Faber. She was tall and wiry with a lot of dark hair pulled back in a ponytail. She was also a lefty.

She fouled off two fastballs, then fouled out to Andy near the stands. What a relief. It looked as if Justin had finally settled down, but not so fast. Catcher Jack Ferraro went the opposite way and scorched the ball down the right field line. Pete was too big and heavy to get there quickly, and Lord was very fast. He scored from first before Pete could get the ball back to the infield, and Ferraro got to second.

Coach Channing came out to the mound. Luke was right behind him, along with Phil and Brian.

Michael got nervous. Would they take Justin out? He didn't think they would—not now, not yet—especially because Justin almost always kept getting better, inning after inning.

Michael saw Justin nod. Then Coach Channing nodded, too, and patted Justin on the shoulder. The group at the mound broke up. Justin would stay in the game. Now he had to get that elusive third out.

He promptly did. He struck out the third baseman, Larry Jordan, and ended the threat.

Now the Rockets came to bat. The crowd was starting to stir again. The score was 3–0 Panthers, but it was only the bottom of the first. From deep in left field came a rousing *Rah! Rah! Rockets!*

On the bench, Michael watched Angela Faber warming up. He listened to the comments Luke and Brian were making.

"Looks like good stuff."

"Lots of heat."

"Think she has a change-up?"

"Yeah. Watch the fingers come up behind the ball. There it is."

"Big wind-up. Maybe she even has a curve."

"Doubt that, but she may not need it."

"We're going to need some luck."

They didn't get it in the first inning. Angela Faber was sharp as a tack. She threw almost nothing but heat, mixing in the occasional change-up just to keep the hitters honest. Luke grounded out to the mound, Phil struck out, Andy bounced to the second baseman, and that was it.

5. In the Clutch

But Justin really had settled down. Nothing much happened until the top of the third when Chuck Reese crushed a deep fly to center with Freddie Berman on first after a lead-off walk.

Michael didn't know how to react. If the ball went out, it meant two more runs. But did he really want Adam to make a spectacular catch and look great?

The crowd was cheering. Adam went way back. He leapt, stuck up his glove, and the ball caught in the webbing before it could go over the fence!

At first he hardly seemed to know what had happened. Then he found the ball and made a good throw to Vicky to hold Berman at first.

The crowd went wild. *Rah Rah Rockets!* they yelled. *Rah Rah Rockets!*

Adam's terrific play seemed to take the

stuffing out of the Panthers. Faber and Ferraro went down in order. The Rockets came to bat.

As Adam reached the dugout, everyone was there to high-five him. Michael thought that better include him too. He offered his high-five and said, "Good going, Adam."

Adam said nothing. He was so carried away with what he'd done, he hardly noticed who had spoken to him.

He was also leading off in the bottom of the third. His newly found self-confidence carried over to his at bat. With the count 1 and 1, he smashed a base hit up the middle. Then he raced to second on Vicky's slow roller to third.

But Vicky was out at first on the only play Larry Jordan had. Then Luke struck out swinging, and Phil lined to short.

But Justin was pitching well now, too. If it hadn't been for that messy first inning, this would have been a real pitcher's duel.

No more runs scored until the top of the sixth. Then, unfortunately, Justin got burned again. Ben Lord led off with a bloop single to left, Angela Faber dropped a perfect bunt down the third base line that sacrificed him to second, and with two out and a full count, he scored on left fielder Cindy Beranski's bouncer over Andy McClellan's head.

Justin stayed in the game. Coach Channing didn't even make a trip to the mound. There was no further damage, but with the Rockets coming in for their last licks in the bottom of the sixth, things didn't look good. The Panthers led 4–0. Angela Faber seemed to be working on a complete game shutout.

Vicky was the lead-off hitter. She stood in and waited Faber out. Ball 1. Ball 2. Strike 1. When the count reached 3 and 1, she got her pitch, a fastball at the letters. She'd noticed that the Panthers were playing her to pull to left, so she turned her shoulder to the right and punched a base hit through the hole!

"Yay, Vicky!" Michael yelled.

The crowd was on its feet, cheering and chanting *Rah Rah Rockets!* It was time for the rally.

Obviously Faber was tiring, but could the Rockets turn it around? Clearly the Panther coach had no intention of going to the bullpen. This game was Faber's to win or lose.

Luke stepped into the batter's box.

"Remember, wait for your pitch!" Coach Carr yelled from third.

Luke did. With the count 2 and 2, he lashed a double over Freddie Berman's head, scoring Vicky on a bad throw to the plate.

Bye, bye, shutout! Then Phil singled to left, scoring Luke, and Andy delivered a chopper down the first base line that scooted into right field and brought Phil over to third.

Was this too good to be true? Two runs were in. There were Rockets on first and third and nobody out.

Justin strode to the plate. He and Brian were the best clutch hitters on the team, and here was his chance to help himself. But Faber had regained her composure, and Justin was trying too hard. She threw two strikes and a ball, then got him swinging on a change-up down and away.

Now it was Brian's turn, and he came through—a single up the middle that scored Phil and sent

Andy roaring in to third. Score: 4–3. Runners again on first and third. Still only one out.

And up came Pete Wyshansky, big Pete, lumbering to the plate with trouble on his mind. But wait! Coach Channing was calling Pete back. He was signaling for Michael to pinch-hit!

Michael was overwhelmed. At this point he hadn't expected to play at all. And why was he pinch-hitting for Pete? No one ever pinch-hit for him.

Then he remembered. Pete had struck out twice today. He'd made two costly errors in the field. This wasn't the time to have someone off his game in the batter's box.

Quickly Michael tried to loosen up. It was a long time since warm-ups, and he'd been sitting on the bench for almost all of it. He put the doughnut on his bat and took a few swings. Then he took a few more swings without the doughnut and walked to the plate.

He passed Pete on the way. Pete didn't even acknowledge him.

Angela Faber looked even more dangerous from the batter's box. As Michael stepped in, he took a deep breath. The game was on the line, and the coach had called on him.

Faber's high leg kick threw off his timing. Before he knew it, the count was 0 and 1, then 1 and 1.

"Stay in there!" Vicky yelled from the bench.

"Come on, Michael!" yelled Justin.

Michael checked the sign with Coach Carr at third. Touch cap. Hit away. He had to drive Andy in from third, put the winning run in scoring position.

"Eye on the ball!" someone shouted, and in it came. A high fastball a little outside, right on the corner. It was his pitch to hit, but for some reason, Michael thought *bunt*. The infield was in, he had to move the runners; a bunt down the first base line would be completely unexpected.

He squared around, reached out, and bunted the ball into the air! It was an easy out for Chuck Reese, coming down the line from first, and of course the runners had to hold.

Michael was devastated. He practically crawled back to the bench. Not only had he not

34

done the job, he hadn't even done what he was supposed to do.

He sat with his head in his hands. He hardly even reacted when Jenny grounded to Max Hobart at short and sealed the Rockets' loss 4–3.

6. After

A hush fell over the dugout. The players seemed to be moving in slow motion as they collected their gear and got ready to go home. They'd shaken hands with the Panthers at home plate, but coming as close as they had at the end, this loss was especially hard to take.

Before anyone could actually depart, Coach Channing had an announcement. "You guys played your hearts out. I'm proud of every one of you. Remember, we have a game against the Titans in Bradford tomorrow. Please be there by one-thirty."

Michael wasn't so sure the coach was proud of him. What, exactly, was there to be proud of? The disregarded sign? The failed bunt? At least no one had said anything mean to him, but then, no one had said anything at all.

He returned to his familiar spot on the bench to wait for his father. What could he say to him?

Jenny sat down, too. "So, trooper, let me guess. You're not very happy."

"Right the first time."

"You saw I made the last out?"

"Yes."

"So shouldn't you be as upset for me as for yourself?"

"Jen, I—"

"I know, I know, it was your only chance and you blew it. But this isn't the end, Michael. The coach isn't going to exile you to the moon."

"I don't know. Do you think they have a baseball team on the moon?"

Jenny laughed. "Sure, only they don't play baseball. They play moonball."

"I bet those little moons are hard to hit."

Michael was chuckling now, too, but at that moment, Adam said to Phil, "Well, at least *I* made a couple of good catches and got a good hit."

It was a low blow. Jenny and Michael shared a look.

Michael glanced up. Wearing a patterned sweater, gray slacks, and very shiny black shoes, his father stood waiting outside the dugout.

"I guess I have to go," Michael said.

"If you want, my dad will drive you to the game tomorrow with Justin and me."

For a moment Michael wondered if he would even go. Then he said, "I'd like that."

"Great! We'll pick you up at one."

"Thanks, Jen."

He joined his father, who said at once, "I'm glad I came. I'm sorry the team lost."

Michael shrugged. "It happens."

As they strolled through the parking lot and out onto Market Street together, Michael congratulated himself on his nonchalance, all the while feeling he was about to come apart.

They walked in silence, turning off Market Street in the direction of their neighborhood, Forest Glen. As they reached the top of their hill, Michael's father said, "Would it have been better if you'd hit the ball harder?"

Michael smiled at his interest. "It would have been a whole lot better," he admitted.

At home he went straight to his room. He couldn't bear to face his mother, his sister, or his brother. Through the closed door, he could hear his father in the kitchen, obviously explaining what had happened.

A while later, there was a knock. "Michael, dinner is ready," said his mother.

He came to the door. "Could I have it on a tray like last night, please?"

"Aren't you feeling well?"

"Just tired."

"Okay, but only if you take a shower first."

Michael looked down and laughed. He'd been in his room for an hour but still had on his Rockets uniform. "Of course," he said, and laughed again.

After showering and eating his dinner, he went to bed. He buried his face in the pillows. Last night he had said he was coming back. Now he was going to have to come back again!

7. Michael's Better!

Promptly at one o'clock, Jack Carr pulled up in the station wagon. Michael was ready. He waved good-bye to his parents, ran down the front steps, and leaped into the backseat beside Jenny. Justin was in front beside his father.

"Hi," said Jenny.

"Hi," said Michael.

The station wagon pulled away. Michael waved again. This morning his father had explained he couldn't come to Bradford. He had to complete plans for an apartment building by tomorrow. They would take the whole day.

He was sorry. He would come the next time.

Michael had said he understood and thought he did. But he couldn't help wondering whether the decision had anything to do with not starting and a poor performance yesterday.

Jack Carr waited at the entrance to the interstate, then slid easily into a break in the traffic. As the station wagon settled into the middle lane, the three ballplayers began a conversation about the Titans, whom they had beaten in their first home game of the season.

Suddenly Jenny leaned forward, balancing her chin on the seat in front. "Justin," she said, "don't you think Michael's better than Adam Spinelli?"

Justin turned his head. "How do you mean?"

"What do you mean how do I mean? Hitting, running, defense. Michael's had a few bad breaks lately, but isn't he better?"

Michael was embarrassed. Why was Jenny doing this?

"Oh, Jen, I don't know," Justin said. "Adam's been playing well lately, but—"

"But. The but means Michael is better. Right?"

"Well, yes, I think so, over all."

"There. You hear that, Michael? Justin thinks you're better, too. Dad, don't *you* think Michael's better than Adam?"

Coach Carr kept his eyes on the road. "I

can't say anything about that, Jenny. Coach Channing wouldn't like it.''

''But Justin thinks Michael is better, and I think Michael is better. Isn't that enough for you to ask Coach Channing to put Michael back on the starting team?''

Coach Carr shook his head. ''You know I can't do that. Coach Channing makes all those decisions himself.''

Jenny leaned back and frowned. Then she whispered, ''At least you know Justin and I think you're better.''

Michael smiled at her. He was no longer embarrassed. He was glad to have a friend like Jenny.

They reached Bradford and then, a few blocks from the interstate, the Titans' field. It was a beauty. Freshly mown grass. Soft dirt on the base paths. A manicured pitcher's mound. Real seats in the stands!

Since the Carrs had made an extra stop for Michael, just about everyone on the team was there ahead of them. Within a few minutes, Coach Lopez was leading them in their warm-ups, and

when the Titans had finished practicing, the Rockets raced out onto the field.

With the other outfielders, Michael began shagging fly balls. As he made an easy catch and pegged the ball back to Coach Carr, Pete walked over to him.

"You creep," he said in a low voice, "if I'd been up yesterday, we would have won the game."

At first Michael was afraid. Pete was a lot bigger than he was. Then he put aside the fear. "Buzz off, Pete!" he said, and ran down another fly ball.

8. Revenge?

But there was no point in being foolish. When Michael returned to the visiting team dugout and learned that both he *and* Pete were not starting, he took care to sit a good distance away from him.

The game began slowly. Little Josh Rubin was pitching for the Rockets (which explained why Andy, number three hitter and top man in the rotation, had replaced slumping Pete in right field). The Titan hitters had seen Josh's crazy sidearm motion back in Raymondtown, but in that first game of the season, they'd only seen it for two innings of relief. It took them a little time to adjust.

At the same time, the Rockets were making adjustments of their own. They'd been expecting to face hard-throwing Jake Thornton, the big, tough black kid who'd almost beaten them before. Instead, Thornton was playing right field, and they were seeing Darryl Jameson, another, smaller, black kid who threw hard but liked to paint the corners of the plate.

Nothing happened for the first two innings, but each time the Rockets left for the field, Pete sidled over to Michael, squeezed his shoulder, and whispered, "Crummy pinch-hitter!" Each time Michael pushed him away and frowned.

Just like in the last game, things got moving in the top of the third. Adam Spinelli led off, waited on a fastball, and doubled to the left field corner. He was so pleased, he jumped up and down on the bag. Then Vicky singled him home, and Adam was high-fived as he reached the plate.

"Yes!" he shouted, "I did it!"

Michael wasn't impressed. He remembered how Adam had bragged about his own performance yesterday, even after the team had lost.

But Luke fouled off two fastballs, then doubled off the center field fence to drive in Vicky. After Phil struck out and Andy flied out, Justin lashed the first pitch to the gap in right center field. Luke came chugging in to score, and Justin ended up on third.

That was all, but the Rockets took the field leading 3–0!

Michael pounded the pocket of his glove. Last time they were behind 3–0 in the third and had to play catch-up ball. Now they could bear down and capitalize on their lead.

And Josh was really rolling. He had good stuff and good control. He struck out the left fielder, Hank Northrop, and the second baseman, Ryan Wildman. Then he faltered for a moment and walked first baseman Andrea Stein.

The next batter was Tommy Chin, the Titans' rugged little shortstop. He hunkered down, let Josh throw two by him, then stepped into a change-up and lifted a towering fly to left-center.

It was very deep. Adam ran—and misjudged the ball completely. He got there late, turned and leaped, but it was over his head and caromed off the fence.

He ran it down, picked it up, and panicked. He overthrew the cut-off man, Brian Krause, and the ball bounced into the dugout. By the time Justin recovered it, Stein had scored and Tommy Chin was on third.

A moment later, Chin scored easily on a shot so deep in the hole at short that Brian had all he could do to smother it. He had no play.

But Josh still had some fire left. Two searing sidearm fastballs followed by a change-up produced a slow grounder to Vicky that ended the inning. The Rockets were still leading 3–2, but they couldn't be very comfortable.

Adam didn't look like a happy camper as he trudged in from center field. He spoke to no one and slumped on the bench, but with Josh leading off, he was due up next. As Josh walked to the plate, Adam took his place in the on-deck circle.

He fiddled with the doughnut, took a few meager swings. When Josh popped up to third, he slouched into the batter's box.

He looked like a sure strikeout. He failed to anchor his back foot, didn't bring his arms back far enough, hardly seemed to be concentrating. Somehow, miraculously, he walked on four pitches. Jameson, who had been painting those corners, started missing them.

''Hey!'' Adam yelled as he jumped on first base. Every player on both teams turned to look at him. ''Hey, drive me in!''

Then he danced off the bag several times, annoying Jameson and provoking a throw.

After Vicky struck out, Adam got what he wanted. Luke slashed a double deep to left. Clearly the runner on first would score. Adam careened around the bases and crossed the plate with his hands over his head as the throw came in wild.

The Rockets had an insurance run, but not for long. Big Jim Jacoby, the Titans' third baseman, called time and gestured to the umpire. He claimed the baserunner had never touched third base!

The umpire considered and nodded. Jameson tossed the ball to Jacoby, who stepped on third.

''You're out!'' the umpire said, and returned to his position behind the plate.

Coach Channing rushed to protest, but it was no use. Their bats cooled, the Rockets returned to the field.

But Adam wasn't done yet. The Titans went down in order in their half of the fourth, and neither team scored in the fifth. Josh almost got burned on a couple of hard hit balls, but he got off the hook when Brian came in in relief. As the Rockets came up in the top of the sixth, the score was still 3–2.

Quickly Jenny flied out to short left, Josh got on on an error by Jacoby, and Adam blooped a checked-swing base hit to right. He was so excited, he made the turn at first and went for two.

What he hadn't noticed was that Josh had stopped at second and was standing on the bag!

He was more than half-way there when he looked up. It was too late. He stopped in his tracks and was easily tagged out in a rundown. The Titans came to bat with the score still 3–2.

Brian gave up a lead-off single and a walk, then uncorked a wild pitch with two out. With runners on second and third, the crowd went wild, cheering for their Titans. Fortunately, Brian struck out Thornton swinging. The Rockets had their victory.

As everyone finished their high-fives and

hugs and got ready to go, Pete slugged Michael on the arm and said again, "Crummy pinch-hitter."

Considering that neither one of them had played in today's game, it was too much. "Cut it out, Pete, if you know what's good for you!" Michael said, and slapped his hand away.

Coach Channing overheard. "Pete," he said, "we'd better have a few words," and led him off.

Of course Michael wanted to listen in, but at that moment he noticed Adam over by the backstop. His father was standing in front of him, shouting and waving his hands.

When the storm ended, Adam said, "I have to get my stuff, Dad."

As he reached the dugout, Michael went over. He'd hated Adam all day long, but now he felt sad for him.

"I'm sorry you had such a terrible day," Michael said.

Adam looked up. "Yeah, I bet you are. You can't wait for the coach to give you back your position."

Michael didn't know how to reply. He wanted to say something about Adam's father but could not. "My position has nothing to do with it," he said.

Adam smirked and turned away. "Sure. Thanks for the kind words."

9. Working for It

Adam had always been a pretty good kid. Transformed into a starting center fielder, he'd become a first-class pill.

Driving back in the station wagon, Michael had time to wonder about this as Jenny and Justin went over the game and the way Adam had almost cost them the win.

"How could he have missed third base?" Jenny asked.

"How could he have gone to second on that bloop single?" was Justin's reply.

"Dad," Jenny asked, "isn't it clear now that Michael should be back in center field? We *need* him there."

"Well, Jenny—"

"Come on, Dad!"

Hands on the wheel, Coach Carr cleared his throat. "I'll put in a good word."

"Hooray!" Jenny yelled, slapped Michael's hand, and fell against the backseat in triumph.

Michael loved it. He slapped Jenny back, and together they giggled quietly for a while. Wouldn't it be great if Coach Carr really said something to Coach Channing?

At home Michael avoided going into details. He just said that the Rockets had won. Who had started in center field and whether he'd played at all never came up.

The next day was Monday and school. Michael was in Mrs. Carey's third grade class, along with Brian and Vicky and a few other members of the Rockets. Most of the team was in Mrs. Irvington's class across the hall, but Michael didn't mind the way he knew Brian did. He really liked Mrs. Carey, and he liked her class.

Unfortunately, one of those other Rockets in Mrs. Carey's class was Adam Spinelli.

The moment Michael arrived, he noticed Adam moping in the back of the room. It was almost as if he were hiding when there was no place to hide.

Michael thought about going up to him, saying something kind. Then he remembered what had happened in Bradford and decided against it.

He went to his seat and zipped through the day feeling pretty good. He answered several questions in math and in language arts, romped through gym and recess, and played his recorder in music. Of course he did find himself going out of his way to avoid Adam, but that wasn't very difficult. Adam seemed to be going out of his way to avoid everyone.

Even at lunch this seemed true. Michael was chatting with Jenny when he noticed Luke, Phil, and Brian hunched over in conversation across the cafetorium. Adam sat off to one side, staring at the wall, not even listening.

Almost at once, the day was over. Michael had some homework, but he wasn't concerned. He'd get through that easily and on to practice after school tomorrow. He couldn't wait to get back on the field and prove himself again.

He breezed through school on Tuesday. A little extra time had restored some of Adam's spirits, but Michael didn't even notice. He just got through, got out, changed his clothes, got down to the ballfield, and performed.

Fly balls caught over the throwing shoulder, the throw low and perfectly timed for the relay man. Grounders fielded easily on one knee with no one on base, charged and gobbled up on the run when there were bases occupied. Always keeping the knees bent, the bottom down, the feet wide apart, the shoulders facing the ball. Always on the balls of the feet and backing up every outfield play, even when it was Pete's. Thanks to the coach, Pete seemed to have decided to leave him alone. That was just fine with Michael.

Then hitting. He settled into the batter's box, anchored his back foot, felt good and relaxed and easy. Right away he started making contact, parking the ball in left and center and left-center, doing what he did best and doing it pitch after pitch. His swing was level, he snapped his wrists, and the ball traveled. For a while anyway, he felt in a groove.

When practice ended, Michael was sweaty

and breathless. With the others, he stood around the mound as Coach Channing announced: "A change in plan. There will be no practice tomorrow. Instead, we will play the Pelicans at three-thirty. It's just a schedule change. We were supposed to play them Saturday. Andy will pitch."

A game tomorrow! Michael thought. Was it too much to hope that Michael Wong might start?

10. The Best Reward

He got to the ballfield early. He couldn't wait to warm up. When he finished warming up, he couldn't wait to get out in the field in his uniform.

A mid-week game meant a small crowd, but there were people in the stands nevertheless, and already they were cheering and chanting and urging on their Rockets. As the Pelicans went out to take practice, Michael's stomach did a flip. Coach Channing was about to post the lineup.

As usual, he waited until last. Then he crept forward and looked.

Pete was back in right. Jenny was in left, and Adam was batting eighth and starting in center field!

Michael was so shocked he was speechless. With all the blunders Adam had made, how

62

could he be starting? Even horrible Pete was starting again. It wasn't fair.

He sank to the bench, humiliated. Jenny was right there beside him. "It's okay, trooper, I know how you're feeling. You'll be starting again soon. I know you will."

Michael shook his head. "Never," he said into his shirt. "Never."

The Rockets were wary of the Pelicans because they had lost to them in Healesville not so long ago. But Andy came out really smoking. The fastball sizzled, and the change-up dove. He mowed down the first two hitters, then closed out the inning with a harmless ground ball to Phil at third.

As the Rockets came to bat, their fans cheered louder.

But the Pelican pitcher was Herb Kelly, the same rugged righthander the team had faced before in relief. The bench got very quiet as Luke led off.

He stepped in, got ready. Then he belted the first pitch over the left field fence!

The crowd roared. All the kids on the Rocket

bench were on their feet. As Luke circled the bases pumping his fist, his teammates applauded. When he reached home plate and stamped on it, they were there with their high-fives.

How sweet it was, but especially for Luke. Herb Kelly had tormented him more than anyone last time out. It was the moment to get something back.

The moment didn't last. No one else could do anything against Kelly, who seemed to grow stronger and more confident from batter to batter. It was almost as if Luke's homer had shocked him into perfect control.

But Andy was not giving up any ground either. In the top of the second, he allowed only one base hit. Then, in the bottom of the inning, Brian managed to walk and steal second before there were two out.

At that point Adam came up. He settled in, trying to look mean and tough. But he'd never faced Kelly before, and he was overmatched. Kelly reared back and started throwing strikes. He struck out Adam on three pitches.

Adam stood at the plate. The frustration tied his face in knots. "Ohhhhh!" he shouted, and hurled his bat against the backstop.

The umpire stepped forward. "You're outta here!" he yelled, and Coach Channing rushed forward to lead Adam away.

But Adam's father arrived at the same instant. There was a brief exchange, and Adam and his father disappeared toward the parking lot.

The stands had grown quiet in disbelief. As Coach Channing returned to the dugout, he said, "Okay, Michael, take over in center field."

Was this really happening? Michael picked up his glove and raced to the outfield.

It had never felt so good. He was announced, the crowd cheered, and the very first batter hit the ball right at him. He made the catch and threw smartly to Vicky at second. It seemed like a good omen.

The Pelicans failed to score in the top of the third, but so did the Rockets in the bottom, despite Phil's sharp single to left. Andy was getting more confident, but Kelly was matching him pitch for pitch. It looked as if the only difference in the game might turn out to be Luke's lead-off home run.

There was a hint of danger in the top of the fourth. With no one out, Kelly singled to right and took second when Pete mistakenly threw behind the runner to first.

Andy was mad about Pete's error, but he wasn't too pleased to have that baserunner dancing off the bag behind him, either. He pounded the ball into his glove, then whirled and picked Kelly off second.

"Good going, Andy!" said Brian.

"Great play!" yelled Phil.

Of course the crowd screamed its head off. Andy got so pumped, he struck out the catcher, Lane Rudolph, got the third baseman, Sherry Kouveras, on a high bouncer to the mound, and walked off the field without a backward glance.

Then, in the bottom of the fourth, Kelly's fastball began losing its pop. Getting picked off might have discouraged him, but whatever it was, Justin singled to right and went on to second as Johnny Martinez overthrew the second baseman. Would the Rockets put something together? Brian lined to third, but Pete managed to squeeze out a walk by holding off on a 3 and 2 pitch before Jenny went down swinging.

Two on, two out. Coming to the plate was Michael Wong.

Michael remembered Kelly from the last time, when he hadn't had a hit. The first pitch was by him for a strike.

But he was seeing the ball well. He crouched a little more and challenged Kelly by leaning out over the plate, hoping the pitch would be outside.

But Kelly crossed him up. The next pitch was a fastball over the inside corner for strike 2.

An 0 and 2 count, and Michael was deep in a hole. But he didn't lose his courage and didn't back off. He got ready, concentrated very hard, and watched another fastball all the way in. Then he swung, met the ball, and put it into left over the shortstop's head.

Justin raced in from second, and the Rockets led 2–0!

In a game dominated by such quality pitching, an insurance run made all the difference in the world. Taking his lead off first, Michael smiled.

The Pelicans changed pitchers. They brought in a lefty, George Nayar, and he put out the fire. But Andy was still surging, and nothing more happened until the top of the sixth when Dixie Rothwell walked and Nayar himself came up with two outs.

He had a broad chest and black hair. Andy hadn't seen him before, and he got nervous. He served up three balls before Nayar snapped his wrists and lined one into center field.

Nayar ran for first as Dixie Rothwell went to second. "Keep going!" he shouted, and there was the Pelican third base coach windmilling her along.

Rothwell rounded second and headed for third as Michael, running hard, snared the ball on the short hop, set, and threw a perfect strike to Phil. Rothwell got nailed, and the umpire yelled "You're out!"

The game was over. The Rockets had won 2–0.

Michael couldn't believe he'd made that throw. Phil, Brian, and Jenny carried him into the dugout, and everyone high-fived him, in-

cluding Luke, who smiled and said, "You proved your point, my man."

When the celebrating had died down, Coach Channing took Michael aside. "You've done an excellent job," he began, "and I don't mean just this afternoon. The way you worked in practice, the way you tried to help Adam even though he was your replacement—I had to be proud of you, Michael. Adam and his dad will need a few lessons in sportsmanship. You're my starting center fielder."

Basking in his coach's praise, Michael looked up. His father was waiting near the dugout.

He had taken time from his work to come to the game. He had seen what Michael had done. It was the best reward of all.